Pearl's
Lost Pearls

Olivier Dunrea

Clarion Books

An Imprint of HarperCollinsPublishers

Library of Congress Control Number: 2023943608
ISBN 978-0-54-786758-8

Typography by Stephanie Hays
24 25 26 27 28   RTLO   10 9 8 7 6 5 4 3 2 1

First Edition

For the Pearls in Worcester—Dot, Lynn, and Mary—the most precious gems I know

This is Pearl.

Pearl is the smallest gosling
with the biggest voice.

Pearl loves wearing pearls.

She wears them everywhere.
Every day.

She wears her pearls when she swims.

She wears them when she
sings to the bees.

Pearl loves loves LOVES her pearls!

She wears them everywhere.
Every day.

She wears them when she dances
on top of the stone wall.

She wears them when she
naps on the haystack.

She wears them when she
sings in the rain.

She wears them everywhere.
Every day.

Pearl loves loves LOVES her pearls!

She even wears them when
she dives in the pond.

After a busy day, Pearl hops home.

"Pearl, where are your pearls?"
asks Papa Goose.

Pearl's pearls are lost!

Pearl is devastated.

She searches in the rain.
No pearls.

She searches under the haystack.
No pearls.

She searches over the stone wall.
No pearls.

She searches around the beehive.
No pearls.

Pearl searches in the pond.
No pearls.

Pearl quietly sits on the pond.
Heartbroken.

Ruby and Rufus have been
diving in the pond too.

They swiftly swim to Pearl.
"Look what we found!"

This is Pearl.
Singing in her pearls!